Girls Don't Have Cooties

D1486641

For Bonnie and Emily

Library of Congress Control Number: 2002106663

ISBN 0-448-42705-2   K L M N O P Q R S T

Girls Don't Have Cooties

by Nancy Krulik • illustrated by John & Wendy

Grosset & Dunlap

Chapter 1

"Here comes Jeremy," Suzanne Lock said. She looked out across the school playground. She quickly handed her best friend Katie Carew an envelope. "Put this in your backpack, fast!"

Katie looked at the envelope curiously. "What's the big secret?" she asked.

"It's an invitation to a party, this Saturday, at my house," Suzanne quickly explained.

"Oh," Katie answered. "So why do I have to hide it from Jeremy? Just give him his invitation too."

Suzanne shook her head. "Jeremy's not invited. No boys are. It's just for the *girls* in our class."

Katie was shocked. "You mean you're only asking half of our friends to your party? You can't do that. We've been friends with Jeremy forever."

Suzanne shook her head. "Jeremy's *your* best friend, Katie, not mine," she insisted. "I only hang out with him when you're around."

Katie couldn't argue with that. It was true. Jeremy Fox and Suzanne were both Katie's best friends. The two of them got along okay when they were with Katie. But Jeremy and Suzanne didn't always like each other.

"What kind of party is it?" Katie asked.

"A sleepover!" Suzanne told her excitedly. "I'm going to rent some movies. We'll do each other's hair and play games. My mom even said we can put on makeup—if we wash it off before we go to sleep." Suzanne flashed Katie a secret smile. "Of course, we're not going to sleep at all. Who sleeps at a sleepover?"

Katie shrugged. She didn't know how to

answer that. She'd never been to a sleepover party before.

"So, will you come?" Suzanne asked her.

Katie nodded. "Sure. Sounds like fun."

"Hey you guys! What's up?" Jeremy asked as he walked over to where Suzanne and Katie were standing.

Katie quickly stuffed her invitation into her backpack. "Um, *nothing*," Katie murmured.

She suddenly felt a little guilty about Suzanne's all-girl party—even though she wasn't the one who was throwing it.

"I gotta go," Suzanne said quickly. "I need to talk to Mandy and Miriam about something important." She winked at Katie. Katie looked away.

Jeremy laughed as Suzanne walked off. "Suzanne's so funny," he said.

"Why?" Katie asked.

"She's always got something important to tell someone," he said. "Doesn't she ever have *nothing* to say?"

Katie giggled. "Not Suzanne. Even if she did, she'd make a big deal about how she had nothing to say."

Jeremy nodded. Then he changed the subject. "My parents are taking me to the Magic Lamp Amusement Park on Saturday night. We're going to check out that new Lightning Bolt roller coaster. They said I could bring a friend. Wanna come?"

Katie's eyes flashed. The Lightning Bolt was supposed to be an amazing roller coaster. The TV commercials said it has three loops and goes really fast!

"Wow! The Lightning Bolt would be a great one to add to my list!" she exclaimed. Katie was trying to go on at least fifty roller coasters before she became a grown-up. So far she'd been on seven different ones.

"That's what I thought," Jeremy told her.

"I would love to go . . ." Katie began. Then she remembered Suzanne's party. "Except I can't go Saturday night," she finished sadly.

"How come?" Jeremy asked her.

"Well . . . um . . . I . . .er . . ." Katie stammered nervously. "I kind of promised to hang out with Suzanne on Saturday night," she said finally.

That was the truth. Jeremy didn't have to know about the all-girl party.

Jeremy thought about that for a minute. "I guess I can bring two friends."

Katie gulped. She really didn't want to have to tell Jeremy about Suzanne's party. It would only hurt his feelings.

"Suzanne doesn't like roller coasters much," Katie said quickly.

"That's okay. Neither does my mom. They could go on the bumper cars while we're on the Lightning Bolt."

Katie sighed. "Well . . . see . . . Suzanne and I sort of have plans with some of the other girls in the class on Saturday night and . . ."

"What kind of plans?" Jeremy interrupted her.

"It's nothing you'd want to do," Katie insisted.

"What are you doing?" Jeremy asked again.

"Well, Suzanne's having this all-girl party," Katie blurted out finally.

Jeremy pushed his glasses up on his nose and stared at Katie. He looked angry. "How come she's only inviting girls?" he asked.

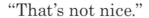

"That's not nice."

"It's a sleepover party," Katie explained. "We're going to put on makeup and do our hair and stuff. You wouldn't want to do that."

"It's still not fair!"

"But Jeremy, it's a *sleepover*!" Katie insisted again. "Boys *can't* come."

Jeremy didn't want to hear it. "Suzanne is being a total snob. She should have a party everyone can come to." He stormed away angrily.

"Where are you going?" Katie called after him.

"I'm going to talk to George and Manny," Jeremy told her. "Wait until *they* hear about this. They're going to be mad!"

Katie played nervously with a lock of her red hair as she watched Jeremy walk away. She had a feeling this was not going to be a good day in class 3A.

Chapter 2

By lunchtime, Jeremy had told all the boys in class 3A about Suzanne's sleepover party. Katie could tell they were mad because they were all sitting together at half of the lunch table. They were also giving the girls really dirty looks.

The girls were sitting at the other end of the table. They were giving the boys dirty looks right back.

By the time Katie reached the lunch table, the only seat left was next to George Brennan and Zoe Canter—right between the girls and the boys. She put her tray down and slid onto her chair.

George jumped up and moved his chair away from Katie. He picked up his hand and made believe he was holding some sort of spray can.

"We want all girls to go away. Blast them hard with cootie spray!" He pretended to spritz Katie all over with invisible spray. "*Pffft*," he said, imitating a spray can.

Katie jumped up with surprise. "George? What are you doing?"

George shrugged. "I'm sorry, Katie Kazoo. But you're a girl. All girls have cooties. I'm

just making sure I don't get them from you."

"What are you talking about?" she asked George.

George moved his chair even farther from Katie. "Oooh! Get this girl away from me!" he shouted. All the boys laughed.

That made Katie upset. George was her friend. He was the one who had given her the nickname Katie Kazoo. They told jokes together and played after school. Katie was the very first kid to become George's friend when he was the new kid at school. Now he wouldn't even sit next to her.

"Come on, George, cut it out!" Katie insisted.

George didn't answer. Instead he took a huge bite of his bologna sandwich and turned toward his buddy, Kevin Camilleri.

"Aachoo!" George let out a really fake sneeze. Pieces of chewed-up bologna, cheese, and bread, sprayed out of his mouth and all over the table.

Kevin chuckled. "Good one, George!"

"Eeeeew! Yuck!" Miriam Chan shouted. She was sitting across from Katie. That gave her a clear view of George's flying food.

"Boys are really gross," Miriam's best friend Mandy Banks said.

"I don't know how you can be friends with any of them, Katie."

Katie sighed. She hated it when there were fights between the boys and the girls.

Just a few weeks ago, Suzanne and Jeremy had had a fight about who would get to take Speedy, the class hamster, home for the weekend. The whole class had gotten involved in that war. The boys had sided with Jeremy, and the girls had sided with Suzanne. Katie had been stuck in the middle—right between her two best friends.

Katie sighed. "I wish this didn't always . . ." Katie was about to wish that this didn't always have to happen to her, but she stopped herself. She'd learned the hard way to be really careful about what she wished for.

It had all started one rotten day. Katie had ruined her favorite jeans, lost the football game for her team, and belched really loudly in front of the whole class. That day, Katie had wished that she could be anyone but herself.

Right after that, the magic wind came.

The magic wind was big and horrible, like a tornado. But it only stormed around Katie. Nobody else could see it or feel it. Whenever the magic wind came, it turned Katie into someone else.

The first time the wind had come, it changed Katie into Speedy, the class hamster! She'd spent a whole morning nibbling on chew sticks and running on a hamster wheel.

Luckily, Katie changed back into herself pretty fast. *Un*luckily, the magic wind had come back again. It turned Katie into Lucille, the cafeteria lunch lady.

But serving mystery meat to her friends wasn't nearly as bad as the next time the wind came. That time it turned Katie into

Suzanne's baby sister, Heather. Katie had come *this* close to having her best friend change her diaper. How embarrassing would *that* have been?

So Katie didn't make wishes anymore. She never knew what would happen if they came true.

Just then, George and Kevin snuck up behind Miriam and Mandy.

"*Pffft!*" the boys shouted. "We want all girls to go away. Blast them hard with cootie spray."

"Get away!" Mandy cried out. "*You're* the ones with cooties."

"No way," George argued. "Girls have cooties."

Katie looked across the table at Jeremy. He was sitting next to Manny Gonzalez. When he saw Katie staring at him, Jeremy looked down at the floor. But Manny didn't look away. He smiled and held up an imaginary spray can. *Pffft.* He pretended to spritz Katie with cootie spray.

Katie was getting mad. *Really mad.*

"*Girls don't have cooties!*" she shouted. Then she jumped up and ran out of the cafeteria.

Chapter 3

"Hey Katie, where are you going?"
Suzanne asked as she ran after her best
friend.

"I can't stand this fighting anymore!"
Katie told her.

"Then stop hanging around with the boys,"
Suzanne suggested. "They started it all."

Katie wanted to tell Suzanne that that
wasn't true. Suzanne had actually started it
all by having an all-girl party. But Katie
already had one best friend refusing to talk to
her. She couldn't take it if Suzanne ignored
her, too.

"Katie, come on outside," Suzanne said.

"We're going to play double Dutch jump rope. Mandy and Zoe have already said that they'll be steady enders."

That was good. Mandy and Zoe were the only ones who knew how to turn both double Dutch jump ropes at the same time without getting them tangled.

"Okay," Katie agreed. "Just let me run back to the classroom and get my jean jacket."

"Great! I'll see ya out on the playground!" Suzanne said with a grin.

$$\times \quad \times \quad \times$$

The classroom was empty. Katie ran in, grabbed her jacket, and headed straight for the door.

But before she could leave the room, she felt a strange breeze tingle against the back of her neck. Katie put on her jacket, and raised the collar around her neck. But she could still feel the breeze blowing.

She looked around the room. The windows

were all shut. The breeze was obviously not coming from outside.

"Oh no!" Katie cried out. "Not again."

The magic wind was back. And she knew there was nothing she could do to stop it.

The wind began to circle strongly around Katie. Her red hair whipped wildly around her head. The tornado swirled faster and faster. Katie held on to a desk so she wouldn't blow away. She closed her eyes tightly, and tried not to cry.

It seemed like the wind was blowing for a very long time. But it was probably just a few seconds before it stopped, just as suddenly as it had begun.

Katie knew what that meant. She wasn't Katie Carew anymore. She was someone else.

The question was, who was she?

Chapter 4

Before Katie opened her eyes, she sniffed at the air around her. The smells had changed. Room 3A smelled like a mix of chalk dust, crayons, and Speedy's hamster litter. *This* room smelled like food—tuna sandwiches, ketchup, french fries, and milk.

Oh, no! This had to be the cafeteria. Had Katie become Lucille the Lunch Lady . . . again?

Slowly, Katie opened her eyes. At first everything looked blurry. Then Katie reached up to her nose and slid her glasses back up toward her eyes.

Glasses? Wait a minute. Katie didn't wear glasses. Who was she?

Katie looked down at her clothes. She was wearing a pair of jeans, black sneakers, and a denim jacket. Typical third-grade clothes.

Okay, so she was a kid. But *which* kid?

Before Katie could figure that out, Kevin poured his chocolate milk onto what was left of his tuna hero. "Hey check this out," he said. "Pretty gross, huh?"

George shook his head. "That's nothing," he said. "Watch this!" He mixed tuna salad into his chocolate pudding and stirred it with ketchup-covered french fries. "Now that's what I call gross!"

Katie looked down at the mess George had just made. It was brown and red, with bits of gray tuna and mayonnaise floating in it. It was possibly the most disgusting thing she'd ever seen.

"See, I told you this was super-colossal-gross," George bragged. "Jeremy looks like he's about to puke just from looking at it."

"I dare you to eat that," Kevin said to George.

That was too much for Katie. If George swallowed a spoonful of that mess she was going to be sick. "No, don't!" she cried out.

George looked over toward Katie. "Relax, Jeremy," he said. "Even I wouldn't eat that mess!"

Jeremy?

Oh, no! Was it possible the magic wind had turned her into her own best friend? Her *boy* best friend?

Of course it was possible. The magic wind could do anything.

"You ready, Captain?" George asked Katie suddenly.

Katie looked back at him. "Ready for what?" she asked, confused.

"The soccer game, remember? You're one of the captains."

"Huh?" Katie asked. "I am?"

"Sure you are," George said. "You're always captain. You're our best player."

"I'm the other captain," bragged Andrew Epstein from class 3B.

"You are?" Katie asked him.

Andrew looked a little annoyed. "We decided this morning, remember?"

"You ready, Jeremy?" Kevin asked Katie. "I want to get out to the field before recess is over."

"Yeah, sure," Katie mumbled nervously. "I think we should go to the bathroom before the game," George suggested. "No time-outs for pee breaks."

"Good idea," Kevin agreed. "Besides, I like the boys' room. No cootie-carrying girls are allowed in there."

Katie gulped. Kevin was right. Not about the cooties, of course. He was only right about girls not being allowed in the boys' room. Boys weren't allowed in the girls' room, either.

Katie wasn't quite sure *which* bathroom she belonged in anymore. After all, she was only Jeremy on the outside. She was still Katie on the inside. The thought of going into the boys bathroom was absolutely, *positively* gross!

Good thing Katie didn't actually *have* to go.

"Not me," Katie said quickly. "You know me, I can hold it forever. I'm like a camel!"

George shrugged. "So you go get the soccer ball. We'll meet you on the field."

Phew! That was close!

Katie had gotten out of that one. But she was pretty sure things weren't going to be that easy once they were out on the field. Katie wasn't a very good soccer player. Her only hope was that Jeremy's body would know what to do once she started playing.

Or, better yet, maybe the magic wind would change her back before the soccer game began.

Chapter 5

"Hey, that took you long enough," Kevin said as he and George caught up to Katie on her way to the soccer field.

Katie was walking very slowly. She was in no hurry to get onto that field.

"Pick me first, Jeremy," George pleaded. "I want to be on your team. Andrew's team never wins."

"Yeah," Kevin agreed. "Andrew and his friends play like girls."

"So what?" Katie asked. "Some girls are great at soccer."

George laughed. "That was funny, Jeremy," he said. "I didn't know you liked to tell jokes."

"I'm not kidding," Katie said.

"Yeah, right," Kevin answered. "Could you just see us playing against the girls? They'd probably want a time-out to fix their hair."

"Or because they broke a nail," George added. He made his voice sound high and squeaky. "Time out for a nail-polish emergency!" he joked.

Katie watched as Kevin and George laughed. They were making her really mad.

Then, suddenly Katie got an idea. *Let them laugh,* she thought to herself. *I'll show them!*

×　　×　　×

"Okay, let's choose up teams," Andrew said, once all the boys were on the soccer field. "Okay if I go first, Jeremy?"

Katie nodded.

"I choose Kevin," Andrew said.

"Oh, man!" Kevin moaned as he moved over next to Andrew.

"I choose George," Katie said.

"Yes!" George cheered. He gave Katie a high-five.

"Now I'll take Billy," Andrew told them.

Katie looked at the crowd of boys standing in front of her. They all wanted to be on Jeremy's team. Slowly she turned to face the playground—where the girls were.

"Hey Mandy!" she called out. "You want to play soccer?"

Suddenly, everything stopped. The girls dropped their jump ropes. The boys stared in surprise.

"Jeremy, what are you doing?" George asked.

"I'm choosing up teams," Katie told him.

"But you can't pick Mandy," George said.

"Why not?"

George looked amazed. "Because she's a girl!"

Katie sighed. "Yeah. But she's also a really good soccer player. Maybe the best in the class. She could win the game for us."

"Sure," George moaned. "We'd win because the other team would be laughing too hard to play!"

"I still choose Mandy," Katie told him.

"I'm not playing with her," George said. "I'm going over to Andrew's team."

"Andrew's team is the *only* team," Kevin said. "No one wants to play with a girl."

"Except Jeremy," Andrew pointed out.

"Jeremy the *girl lover*!" George shouted.

"Girl lover, girl lover!" The other boys began chanting. "Jeremy's a girl lover!"

Kevin lifted his hand and sprayed some imaginary cootie spray. We want all girl *lovers* to go away. Blast them hard with cootie spray!" he shouted.

"Let's get out of here, you guys!" George told the others. "We don't want to get cooties from Jeremy the girl lover!"

The boys ran over to the playground.

"Get 'em!" George shouted, as he ran straight toward Suzanne and blasted her with imaginary cootie spray.

Katie stood alone on the soccer field and watched the boys chase the girls. She'd wanted to fix things between the girls and the boys. That's why she'd picked Mandy for Jeremy's team.

"I hate you, George!" Suzanne cried out.

Katie sighed. Instead things were worse than ever.

Chapter 6

It was lonely on the soccer field. All the other kids were running around on the playground. They didn't even notice that one of their friends was standing there, all alone.

These days, the worst thing any boy in 3A could be called was a girl lover! Katie knew that when Jeremy found out what had happened, he was going to be upset. And it was all Katie's fault.

Usually, when the magic wind turned Katie into someone else, she couldn't wait to become Katie Carew again. But this time was diferent. Katie didn't want to turn back into herself. She wanted to stay Jeremy for a little longer. At least long enough to fix things.

But the magic wind never seemed to care what Katie wanted. Suddenly, a cool breeze began to blow. Katie looked over toward the trees. The leaves were still. She glanced over at the flag post. The flag wasn't moving. *The magic wind was back.*

Once again, wild winds began to circle around Katie. The magic wind was so strong that it whipped off Jeremy's glasses. Katie reached out to grab them, but the glasses flew across the field.

Oh, no! Jeremy wouldn't be able to see without his glasses. Katie tried to run after them. The magic wind wouldn't let her move. It was holding her prisoner.

And then it just stopped. Slowly Katie opened her eyes. She looked around. She was still out on the soccer field.

Okay, so now she knew where she was. But she still didn't know who she was.

Nervously, Katie looked down at her feet.

There were her purple shoes and her pink glitter pants.

She held up her hands. She was still wearing the same electric green, glow-in-the-dark nail polish she'd put on the day before.

Katie was back.

And so was Jeremy Fox. He was standing just a few feet from Katie on the field. Jeremy looked kind of funny without his glasses on. Katie hardly ever saw him like that.

"Where am I?" Jeremy mumbled to himself. He squinted his eyes and tried to find his glasses.

Katie spotted Jeremy's glasses by a tree. She picked them up and handed them to him. "Looking for these?" she asked him.

"What happened?" Jeremy asked. "I mean, I sort of remember coming out here, but . . ."

Katie gulped. How was she going to explain what happened? She couldn't just say that the magic wind had turned her into Jeremy. He'd never believe her. If it hadn't

happened to her, Katie wouldn't believe it,
either.

"What do you mean you 'sort of remember'?"
Katie asked him.

Before Jeremy could answer, George's
teasing voice rang out over the playground.
"Hey! Look at the girl lover talking to Katie
Kazoo!"

Jeremy's face turned beet red.

"Jeremy's a girl lover! Jeremy's a girl

lover!" the boys all began to chant.

Jeremy's put his glasses on and stared at the boys angrily.

"Who are you calling a girl lover?" he asked them.

"You!" Kevin shouted back.

"Who says?" Jeremy asked.

"Hey, you're the one who picked a girl for your soccer team!" Manny told him.

Jeremy looked confused. "What are you talking about?"

"Hello? Aren't you the one who picked Mandy Banks to be on your team?" George asked.

Jeremy thought for a minute. "I think I remember something like that," he began. "I don't know. It's all kind of weird."

"We thought it was pretty weird too," Manny told him.

"*Scary* weird," Andrew added.

"Next thing you know, you'll be putting on a frilly nightgown and going to Suzanne's

dumb old sleepover party," George said. He
pretended to hold up the edges of an invisible
skirt.

Just the mention of Suzanne's party made
Jeremy really mad. There was no way he was
going to be called a girl lover!

"Hey, can't you guys take a joke?" Jeremy
asked.

"Huh?" Kevin asked.

"It was just a joke," Jeremy told them.
"Come on, George. You love jokes. You must
have known I was kidding. I would never play
soccer with a girl!"

George thought about that. "I don't know,
Jeremy. You seemed pretty serious out there."

"I'm not a girl lover!" Jeremy insisted.

Katie couldn't believe her ears. How could Jeremy say that? They had been best friends since they were babies.

Jeremy looked away from Katie's sad, angry eyes. "I wouldn't be caught dead near a girl!" he assured the boys.

"Oh yeah?" Manny asked. "Prove it!"

Jeremy thought about that for a minute. Then he got an idea. "Okay, you guys meet me by the slide after school. Those girls think it's okay to have a party without us? We'll show them!"

Just then, Mrs. Derkman blew her loud whistle. "Class 3A line up!" she called out. "Recess is over."

As the boys raced to line up, George whispered to Jeremy, "This had better be good!"

"Oh it is," Jeremy assured him. "It's *really* good!"

Chapter 7

After school, Katie and Suzanne went to Katie's house. "What do you think the boys are planning?" Katie asked Suzanne as the girls walked into Katie's bedroom.

"Who knows?" Suzanne answered, plopping down on the bed. "Who *cares*? No matter what they're planning, it won't be as fun as my sleep-over party."

Just then Pepper, Katie's cocker spaniel, padded into the room. He hopped up on the bed and licked Katie's face.

"I guess Pepper is the only boy who'll hang out with me anymore." Katie kissed her dog right on his cold, wet nose.

"Blech!" Suzanne exclaimed. "I don't know how you can kiss Pepper. He's got dog breath!"

"It's not so bad," Katie told her.

"I guess not," Suzanne agreed. "It can't be any worse than George Brennan's breath after he eats pickles and Doritos."

Katie laughed. George did eat some weird food combinations. "No, it's definitely not *that* bad. I don't mind kissing Pepper. He's like part of my family."

"Exactly," Suzanne said. "He's not like a human boy. He'd never turn on you the way Jeremy did!"

Katie frowned. She wished Suzanne hadn't brought that up. Jeremy had hurt Katie's feelings—big time.

"Where were you today during recess, anyway?" Suzanne asked Katie suddenly. "You went to get your jacket and then you just disappeared."

Katie didn't say anything. There was no way she could explain what had happened to her.

"Well, you definitely missed it," Suzanne continued. "Nobody could believe it when Jeremy picked Mandy to be on his team. It was really mean of him to tease her like that."

"Are you sure he was teasing?" Katie asked.

"Of course. The boys would never have let her play," Suzanne said.

"But Mandy is a good player," Katie replied.

"I know," Suzanne agreed. "The boys are *afraid* to play against her."

Katie shrugged. "I guess."

Suzanne smiled and pulled a notebook from her backpack. "I don't want to waste one more minute talking about those yucky boys," she said. "I want to plan my sleepover party. It's going to be the best ever!"

Katie listened as Suzanne talked on and on about junk food, movies, and flashlight games. It wasn't all that interesting, but it was better than thinking about what the boys

were planning. There was going to be real
trouble in school tomorrow, and Katie couldn't
help but feel that it was all her fault.

Chapter 8

By the time Katie got to school the next morning, all of the boys in class 3A were already there. They'd gathered under a tree.

Katie walked over to the crowd of boys. "Hey Jeremy, what's going on?" she asked her pal.

Jeremy turned away and didn't answer.

"Come on, Jeremy, cut it out," Katie said. "Answer me."

"Go away Katie," he told her. "You can't be here."

"Why not?" she said.

"Because this is a meeting of the Boys Club," Kevin butted in. *"No girls allowed!"*

"What Boys Club?" Katie asked.

"It's our new club," Manny told her. "We have a club handshake and a club language. They're secret. Only boys can know them."

"Oh, come on guys, we can tell Katie Kazoo," George said suddenly.

"Are you nuts?" Kevin asked him.

"Nah. Katie's cool. We can teach *her* our secret language," George said.

Katie was surprised. She was also happy. Maybe this fighting was finally going to end.

"Yeah, I'm cool," she assured the boys.

"So, repeat after me," George told her. "*Awa.*"

"*Awa,*" Katie repeated.

"*Ta si.*"

"*Ta si.*"

"*Lee goo.*"

"*Lee goo.*"

"*Siam,*" George finished.

"*Siam,*" Katie said.

George nodded. "Good. Now put it all together."

Katie took a deep breath. "Okay, here goes. *Awa ta si lee goo siam,*" she said. All the boys started to laugh.

At first Katie didn't know what was so funny. Then she figured it out. When she said the words all together, it sounded like "Oh what a silly goose I am!"

"Gotcha!" George told her. "We'll *never* reveal our secrets to a girl. Now get out of here!"

Katie choked back the tears as she walked away.

"What's wrong?" Suzanne said when she spotted Katie walking alone on the playground.

"The boys have started a club," Katie told her.

"So what?" Suzanne asked.

"No girls are allowed," Katie explained.

"Like I said, *so what*?" Suzanne said. "We should start our own club. A Girls Club. It'll be so much better than theirs."

Just then, the boys started chanting their new cheer. "Girls go to Jupiter to get more stupider. Boys go to college to get more knowledge!" the boys shouted.

"Oh, please!" Suzanne said. "That is so old. The last time I heard that one I fell off my dinosaur."

Katie didn't laugh. Her feelings were too hurt.

Suzanne smiled and put her arm around Katie. "Come on. Let's get the other girls," she said. "I know we can come up with something better than that!"

Chapter 9

By lunchtime, the all-new Girls Club had its own cheer. "Shout it big! Shout it proud! We're the girls club. No boys allowed. Stomp your feet. Make some noise. Let everyone know. *We hate boys!*" They chanted.

Then the boys started to shout their cheer. "Girls go to Jupiter to get more stupider. Boys go to college to get more knowledge!" They made sure they cheered even louder than the girls.

Soon, both clubs were screaming their cheers. The whole cafeteria heard them. Unfortunately, so did Mrs. Derkman. She blew her whistle loudly.

Everyone stopped screaming. It was the first time Mrs. Derkman had ever blown her whistle *inside*. She must have been really angry!

"That's enough!" the teacher shouted. "There will be no recess after lunch. I want you all to sit here and think about how you are acting."

"That's not fair!" George shouted. "The girls started it!"

Suzanne opened her mouth to argue. Then she saw the look on Mrs. Derkman's face. She closed her mouth.

A few minutes later, class 3A was alone in the cafeteria. Everyone else was playing outside.

"This is so unfair," Mandy moaned. She put her head down on the table.

"If they hadn't started that dumb Boys Club, none of this would have happened," Miriam agreed.

"I wish we could get them back for everything they've done," Zoe added.

Suzanne grinned. "I know how we can," she said. She whispered something to Mandy.

"Great idea!" Mandy agreed.

"What? What?" Zoe asked.

The girls all gathered around Suzanne. All the girls *except* Katie, that is. Katie didn't want to hear Suzanne's latest idea. She knew it would be a mean idea. There had been enough meanness in class 3A already.

For a while all the girls were quiet. They were waiting for Mrs. Derkman to leave the room. As soon as the teacher was gone, Suzanne jumped up. "They're all around us! They're all around us!" she cried out. She looked really scared.

Mandy leaped up. *"Aaaahhh!"* she screamed. "They're all around us!"

George stared at the girls. "What's going on?" he asked nervously.

"Look! They're all around us!" Suzanne
cried out again.

"Oh, no!" Kevin said as he looked under
the table

"Look everywhere. They're all around us!"
Zoe added.

Manny started to cry.

Jeremy pulled his legs up onto his chair.
"*What's* all around us?" he asked nervously.

Suzanne stopped screaming. "The walls.
The walls are all around us!" She laughed so
hard she couldn't stop.

"You big scaredy-cats," Miriam teased.
"You should have seen your faces."

Katie looked at the boys. Their faces
weren't scared anymore. They were angry.

"That was a great one, huh, Katie?"
Suzanne asked her best friend.

Katie nodded. "You really got them," she
said. "But I wonder what they're going to do
to get us back."

Chapter 10

That afternoon, Katie walked home from school by herself. Her mom was waiting for her on the front porch.

"Where's Jeremy?" Katie's mom asked as Katie walked up the stairs to the house.

Katie shrugged. "I have no idea."

Katie's mom seemed surprised. "I thought Wednesday was your special day with Jeremy. You two *always* spend Wednesday afternoons together."

It was true. Most of the other kids had activities on Wednesday afternoons. Suzanne took ballet classes. George and Kevin had tae kwon do. Manny had his piano lessons. But

Katie and Jeremy were always free on Wednesdays. That was their playdate day.

"Jeremy doesn't play with girls anymore," Katie said sadly.

"Oh, I see," Katie's mom said.

"It really stinks!" Katie exclaimed.

"I agree," her mother said. "Maybe he'll change his mind."

Katie shook her head. "I don't think so, Mom. I don't think any of the boys will ever talk to a girl again."

Katie's mom laughed. "Oh, they will. Don't you worry."

Katie sighed. She wished she could believe her mom.

"Do you want a snack?" Katie's mother asked.

Katie shook her head. "I don't feel much like eating."

"So, what do you want to do?"

"There's nothing to do," Katie told her. "I am so bored!"

"Do you have any homework?" her mother asked.

Katie rolled her eyes. How could her mother think about homework at a time like this?

Just then Pepper came running outside. He licked Katie's hand. Katie pet his head but didn't smile. Pepper tugged at Katie's pant leg with his teeth. Katie moved her leg away. Pepper looked up at Katie with his big, brown eyes. He let out a loud bark.

"I think he wants to go for a walk," Katie's mom said finally. "Why don't you take him? It's better than just sitting around here all afternoon."

"I guess," Katie agreed. "Come on, Pepper."

Pepper leaped up and ran eagerly down the block. Katie followed behind him. When they reached the end of Katie's street, Pepper turned right and kept walking. Before Katie realized where she was going, Pepper had led her to Jeremy's house.

Jeremy was out on the lawn playing soccer. Well, not *playing*, actually. He was just sort of dribbling the ball back and forth. That's all you can do when you play soccer alone.

As soon as Pepper saw Jeremy, he raced onto the lawn. Pepper loved playing ball with Jeremy. The cocker spaniel barked excitedly. He used his brown-and-white snout to steal Jeremy's soccer ball and push it across the lawn.

"Hey, cut that out!" Jeremy shouted at the dog.

"Don't you yell at my dog," Katie told Jeremy.

"Then get your dog away from my ball," Jeremy told her. "He's ruining my practice."

"Oh, big deal," Katie argued back. "He's just having fun."

"Well, let him have fun somewhere else. Take him over to one of your *girlfriends'* houses," Jeremy said.

"I would if I could," Katie replied. "No one's home."

"What are you doing here anyway?" Jeremy asked. "Did you come to spy on me?"

Katie frowned. "You're not that interesting."

"Then why are you here?" Jeremy asked. "I was just following Pepper. *He* was the one who came over here. But don't worry, we're leaving."

Katie turned toward her dog. But he wasn't on the lawn. She looked around. Pepper wasn't there.

"He must be in the backyard," Jeremy said.

"You'd better get him before he walks all over my mom's flowers."

"Come on, Pepper," Katie called. But Pepper didn't come.

"Pepper! Here boy!" Katie shouted, louder this time. But the dog still didn't answer her call.

"Pepper!" Jeremy screamed. "Get out here!"

The kids waited a minute. When Pepper still didn't come running, Katie's heart began to pound.

"Oh, no!" she cried. "Pepper's gone!"

Chapter 11

"He probably just went home," Jeremy said. "He knows the way there."

"Maybe," Katie answered hopefully. "I'm going to go check right now." She ran off toward her house.

"Wait up!" Jeremy called after her. "I'll go with you."

They raced to Katie's house. Jeremy searched Katie's yard. Katie ran inside and looked in all the rooms. She wanted to tell her mom what had happened, but she was talking on the phone. So Katie looked under the beds and in the closets all by herself. But Pepper wasn't there.

"This is awful!" Katie cried when she met Jeremy outside. "Pepper's never just run off like this! What if he doesn't know how to get back?"

"That won't happen," Jeremy assured her. "Pepper knows this neighborhood really well. He'll find you."

"We have to keep looking," Katie said. "He's got to be around somewhere."

Jeremy and Katie spent the next hour looking for Pepper. They looked in their neighbors' yards. They peered under bushes

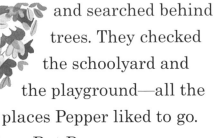

and searched behind trees. They checked the schoolyard and the playground—all the places Pepper liked to go. But Pepper was nowhere to be found.

"Poor Pepper," Katie cried. "He's lost and all alone. He's probably really scared. Oh, Jeremy! What if I never see him again?"

"Someone will find him," Jeremy told her. "He's got all those tags on him. Whoever finds him is sure to call you."

"I have to make signs!" Katie said. "I'll offer a reward for him."

"Come on. Let's go to my house and make some signs," Jeremy suggested.

Katie followed Jeremy home.

"You go sit on the deck in the backyard." Jeremy said. "I'll get paper and markers."

Katie did as she was told. She flopped down in one of the plastic chairs on the deck. She began to sob.

"Oh, *Pepper!* I miss you so much," she cried.

Just then Katie heard a little bark.

"Pepper?" she called out.

There was another little bark. Then Pepper came bounding out from underneath Jeremy's backyard deck. He had an old, soggy tennis ball in his mouth.

Katie sobbed even harder. But this time she was crying tears of joy. She hugged her dog tightly and kissed his little, round head. "Pepper! You're okay!"

Jeremy came out of the house carrying a pile of construction paper and some markers.

"Jeremy, look who's here," Katie exclaimed.

"Pepper! Boy, were we worried about you," Jeremy stroked one of Pepper's long, furry ears. "Where was he?"

"Under the deck, I think. We didn't look there. He might have been there the whole time."

"Why would he go under the deck?"

Katie frowned. "He probably hid there because he couldn't stand us fighting," she said. "He hates when people yell."

"I guess we *were* pretty loud," Jeremy admitted. Then he stopped for a minute and smiled at Katie. "You know, I forgot we weren't supposed to be talking to each other."

"Me, too," Katie said. "I'm really sorry. I mean about Suzanne's party and everything."

"I'm sorry about the Boys Club. It was a dumb idea," Jeremy apologized.

"So, are we friends again?" Katie asked.

Jeremy smiled. "We were always friends," he said.

Katie sighed. "You know, you don't have to talk to me at school or anything if you don't want to. The boys don't have to know we're still best friends."

"That's dumb," Jeremy said. "We can be friends with whoever we want."

"Yeah," Katie agreed.

"The only problem is, everyone else is going to be mad at us for being friends," Jeremy said sadly.

Katie thought about that. Then suddenly she got one of her great ideas. "I know a way we can stop that from happening!" she said excitedly. She grabbed a piece of paper and a magic marker. "Here's what we do . . ."

Chapter 12

Manny, Kevin, and George sure were surprised when they got to school Thursday morning. They found Jeremy sitting under a tree . . . with *Katie*!

"Jeremy!" Kevin exclaimed. "What are you doing with her?"

"I hope you brought along a lot of cootie spray," George added. "She's loaded with them!"

"Cut it out George," Jeremy said. "Katie's my friend. She's your friend, too—in case you forgot."

George covered his ears. "Stop talking like that! That's not how members of the Boys

Club should sound."

"I'm not in the Boys Club anymore," Jeremy told him.

"Why not?" Kevin asked.

Before Jeremy could answer, Suzanne, Miriam, Mandy, and Zoe walked over to the tree.

"Come on, Katie," Suzanne said. "We have a Girls Club meeting now."

Katie shook her head. "I'm not in the Girls Club anymore."

"What?" Suzanne asked with surprise.

"Jeremy and I are starting a new club," Katie explained. "The BUG Club." She held up a picture she'd drawn. It was a picture of a ladybug and a bumblebee.

"The BUG club," George laughed. "That's perfect for girls. The *cootie* bug club!"

"Not funny," Jeremy said. "BUG stands for Boys United with Girls."

"Isn't that BUWG?" Mandy asked.

"I know," Katie admitted. "But that doesn't

spell anything. So we're just calling it the BUG Club."

"I think the BUG Club sounds awful," Suzanne said.

"It's a great club," Jeremy told her. "We're going to do all kinds of fun things."

"And we're not going to fight like your clubs do," Katie added.

"What kind of things are you going to do?" Manny asked.

"Well, for starters, we're going ice skating at Skyrink this weekend," Katie said.

"This weekend?" Suzanne asked. "But my party is this weekend."

"And we were going to go to the amusement park," Manny reminded Jeremy.

"But that's on Saturday," Katie said. "The BUG Club is going skating on Sunday."

"That way we can do everything," Jeremy added.

"It's okay to do things just with girls or boys *sometimes*," Katie said. "But that doesn't

mean we can't all hang out together other
times."

"That's what the BUG Club is all about,"
Jeremy explained. "Everybody being friends."

"Well, ice skating *is* fun," Kevin said.

"I do have this adorable purple skating
dress," Suzanne thought out loud. "It's got
glitter on the skirt."

"The BUG Club, huh?" Zoe said. "That
sounds kind of cute."

Katie looked over at Jeremy and smiled.
The first meeting of the BUG Club was work-
ing out just fine.

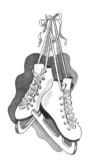

Chapter 13

Katie laughed as she saw George holding onto the side of the rink. He was trying not to fall. He'd never been ice skating before. "Come on George, you can do it!" Katie cheered him on.

George tried to smile. "You know what the hardest part of skating is, Katie Kazoo?" he joked.

"No. What?"

"The ice!" George answered. He rubbed his rear end. George had done a lot of falling today.

Katie giggled. "You're getting better," she assured him.

Suzanne skated up to Katie. "This BUG Club is a lot of fun," she said. "I just wish I wasn't so sleepy."

"You're the one who wanted to stay up all night," Katie reminded her. "The rest of us fell asleep before the movie was over."

Suzanne gave her a tired smile. "I told you. Nobody is supposed to sleep at a sleepover."

Just then, Jeremy shouted across the ice. "Hey everyone, let's do the BUG Club cheer!"

"Yeah!" The kids cried out.

"Buzz, buzz, buzz! Zap, zap, sting! If you're in the BUG Club, friends are everything!"

As Katie listened to her friends cheer, she felt a cool breeze hit the back of her neck. Oh no! Was this magic wind again? Who was she going to turn into now?

Then Katie remembered that she was at an ice-skating rink. The whole room was breezy. She was *supposed* to feel cold.

Katie wrapped her scarf a little tighter around her neck and skated around the rink with her friends. She didn't want to think about the magic wind. She was happy just being Katie.

At least for now.

Jeremy's Soccer Center

If you play soccer or if you want to learn how, this chapter's for you. It's filled with tips from Jeremy Fox—the best soccer player in class 3A.

1. Always warm up before you play. If you don't, you might hurt your muscles. If you're playing on a cold day, do your warm-ups in a sweatsuit to keep your muscles warm. Don't take the sweatsuit off until game time.

2. Don't use your hands (unless you're the goalie).

3. When you're trying to score a goal, where you kick the ball is more important than how hard you kick it. A well-placed shot is more likely to go into the goal.

4. Never turn your back on the ball. Keep your eyes on the ball at all times!

5. If you are a defensive player, it's your job to stay between the ball and the goal whenever you can.

6. If you are a forward, switch positions with the other forwards on your team. For instance, have the left wing switch places with the center. It's a good way to confuse the other team.

7. Always talk to your teammates when you are on the field. Let them know if the ball is coming their way or if someone is sneaking up beside them.

8. If you are a defensive player who is trapped, pass the ball to your goalkeeper for safety. Just make sure your goalie is ready for the pass. You don't want to kick the ball past him and into your own goal.

9. Don't dribble the ball on your own when you can make a safe pass to another player.

10. Always respect the referee's decision. Being a good sport is part of being a great player.